For Bennett and Nora . . . each delightfully *unique!*
LOVE FROM GRANDMA KATIE

For Kyla Ecle . . . *uniquely* beautiful!
LOVE FROM AUNTIE DEBBIE

To Lee Lee and Penny Marie, and also to Cherie, Michelle,
and their *beautiful* baby, with lots of love.
—R. B.

STERLING CHILDREN'S BOOKS
New York

An Imprint of Sterling Publishing Co., Inc.
1166 Avenue of the Americas
New York, NY 10036

Text © 2019 Kathryn Heling and Deborah Hembrook
Illustrations © 2019 Rosie Butcher

ISBN 978-1-4549-2292-6

Distributed in Canada by Sterling Publishing Co., Inc.
c/o Canadian Manda Group, 664 Annette Street
Toronto, Ontario M6S 2C8, Canada
Distributed in the United Kingdom by GMC Distribution Services
Castle Place, 166 High Street, Lewes, East Sussex BN7 1XU, England
Distributed in Australia by NewSouth Books
University of New South Wales, Sydney, NSW 2052, Australia

For information about custom editions, special sales, and premium and corporate purchases,
please contact Sterling Special Sales at 800-805-5489 or specialsales@sterlingpublishing.com.

Manufactured in China

Lot #:
2 4 6 8 10 9 7 5 3 1
02/19

sterlingpublishing.com

Book design by Ryan Thomann
The artwork for this book was created digitally.

There's Only One YOU

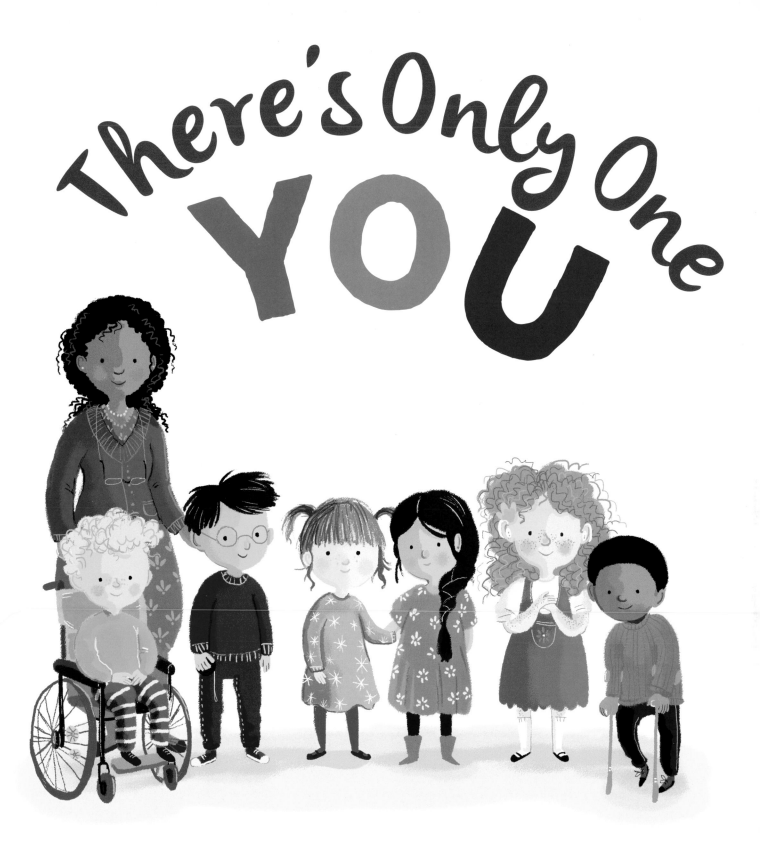

by **Kathryn Heling** and **Deborah Hembrook**
illustrated by **Rosie Butcher**

STERLING CHILDREN'S BOOKS
New York

In all the world over,
this much is true:

You're somebody special.
There's only one you.

Your knees might feel knobby;
your ears might stick out.
Are you tall? Are you short?
Are you thin? Are you stout?

You might be outgoing,
or maybe you're meek.
Whatever—it's awesome,
being unique!

Do your feelings spill out?

Do they lay low and hide?

You might cry when you're sad
or keep tears inside.

Do you smile just a bit
or laugh loud with a shriek?

You're different—it's awesome,
being unique!

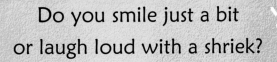

Your color of skin is a beautiful sight,
light as the moon or dark as the night.

Your skin is so perfect,
from toes to your cheeks.
It's truly splendiferous
being unique!

Your hair might be curly
or a long, thick cascade,
worn short in a buzz cut
or tied in a braid.

RING-TAILED LEMUR
(LEMUR CATTA)

Your hair might be poofy,
or straight, smooth, and sleek.

It's wild, it's wonderful
being unique!

TAPANULI ORANGUTAN
(PONGO TAPANULIENSIS)

When there's something to say,
do you talk with your hands?

Do you speak with an accent
from faraway lands?

Some voices are booming,

and some, just a squeak.

Your way is the best way
of being unique!

Can you sing? Do you dance?
Sports and drawing are fun.
Good at spelling or math?
Do you like more than one?

$2 + 2 = 4$
$2 + 4 = 6$
$2 + 6 = 8$

Is building for you?
Or gymnastic techniques?
It's great—celebrate
being unique!

You might have cool glasses
that help you to see.
A wheelchair or walker
gives mobility!

A hearing aid helps you to hear people speak.

Listen! It's glorious being unique!

Friends come in bunches
or groups of a few.
But maybe just one friend
is perfect for you.

Do you play with your friends
once a day? Once a week?
It's fun; it's fabulous,
being unique!

When it's time to dig in
and learn something new,
there's more than one way
of seeing it through.

You can work slow and steady
or in a fast streak.
Your brain grows in **your** way,
being unique!

Families are families,
but soon you will find

that each can be different—
a "best-for-them" kind.

You're part of a family.
You make it complete.

Hurrah for the one that's yours—
it's unique!

In all the world over,
this much is true:

You're special—unique.
There's just one of you!